This

LOVE

...es, Kitty and Flo
IO

For my husband, James
- HL

The Forest Stewardship Council® (FSC®) is an international,
non-governmental organisation dedicated to promoting
responsible management of the world's forests. FSC operates a
system of forest certification and product labelling that
allows consumers to identify wood and wood-based products
from well-managed forests and other controlled sources.

For more information about the FSC,
please visit their website at www.fsc.org

CATERPILLAR BOOKS
An imprint of the Little Tiger Group
www.littletiger.co.uk
1 Coda Studios, 189 Munster Road, London SW6 6AW
First published in Great Britain 2019
This edition published in paperback 2019
Text by Isabel Otter • Text copyright © Caterpillar Books Ltd. 2019
Illustrations copyright © Harriet Lynas 2019
A CIP catalogue record for this book is available from the British Library
All rights reserved • Printed in China
ISBN: 978-1-84857-854-8
CPB/1800/1570/0920
2 4 6 8 10 9 7 5 3

ISABEL OTTER

HARRIET LYNAS

This

LOVE

LITTLE TiGER

LONDON

It doesn't matter who we are,
join hands and stand up tall.
Love is a special language
that's understood by all.

Graceful birds swoop low and dive,

soaring through the air.

We watch in quiet wonder;

a loving moment shared.

We nestle close together in our cosy little nook...

The words
painting pictures

as we share
our favourite book.

We roam the streets as one;

Dog's always at my side.

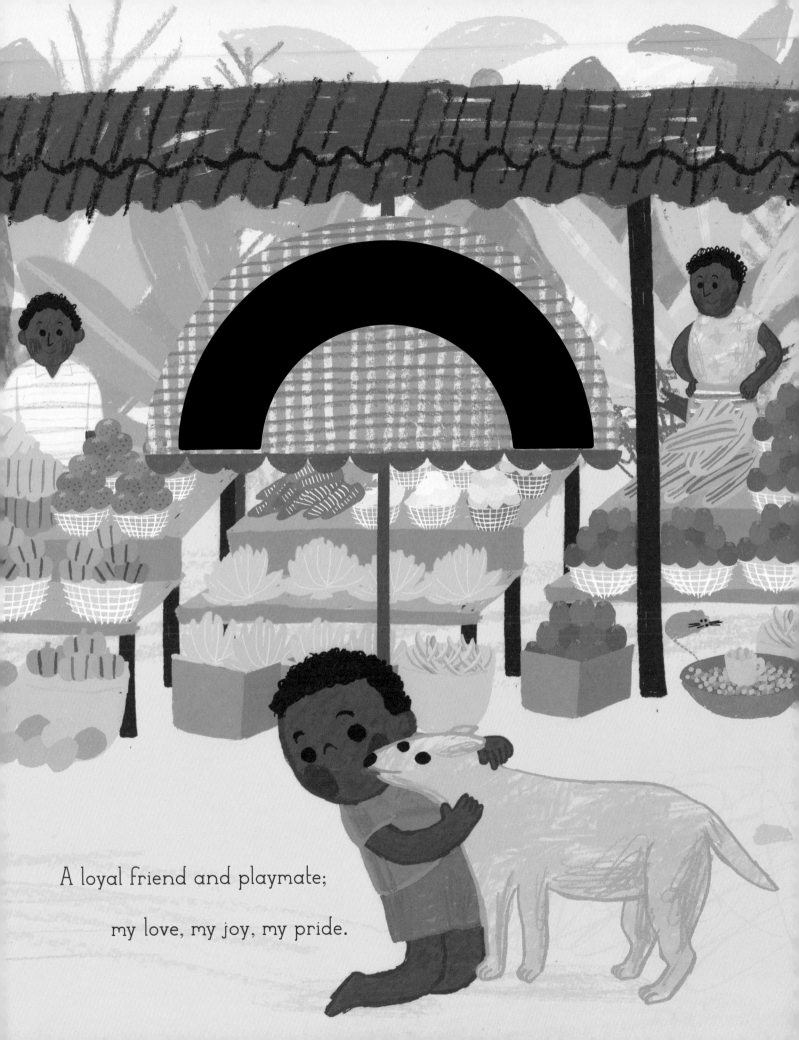

A loyal friend and playmate;

my love, my joy, my pride.

We will laugh and play all day
under stormy skies.

Splish, splash, splosh! We love the rain!

A wonderful surprise.

I watch the crystal carpet form

as balls of snow are flung.

Soft flakes float gently in the air,

then melt on my hot tongue.

Coloured streamers fizz and pop,

lighting up the night.

Goodnight kisses for us all

as sparks fade from sight.

We dig a hole, then scatter seeds

to take care of our land.

My grandpa teaches me to sow
with patient, loving hands.

We'll dance and prance in fountains, make rainbows in the spray.

We love to leap and twirl about, please can we stay all day?

Can you hear a drip, drip, drop?

Rain is falling fast!

And though the seasons come and go, our special bond will last.

Dad's safe hands are guiding me, and now I'm on my own!

I know he's right behind me; I'll never feel alone.

We share our laughter, songs and tales
while parrots preen and call.

The sun is winking on the sea
as dusk begins to fall.

My baby brother has been born,
I must look out for him.
His tiny finger curls 'round mine;
my heart fills to the brim.

It doesn't matter who we are,
join hands and stand up tall.
Love is a special language
that's understood by all.